THE WHALES' SONG

To Isha - D.S.
To Lin - G.B.

1 3 5 7 9 10 8 6 4 2

Copyright © text Dyan Sheldon 1990
Copyright © illustrations Gary Blythe 1990

Dyan Sheldon and Gary Blythe have asserted their rights
under the Copyright, Designs and Patents Act, 1988
to be identified as the author and illustrator of this work.

First published in the United Kingdom 1990 by Hutchinson Children's Books

First published in Mini Treasures edition 1998 by Red Fox
Random House, 20 Vauxhall Bridge Road, London, SW1V 2SA

Random House Australia (Pty) Ltd
20 Alfred Street, Milsons Point, Sydney, New South Wales 2061, Australia

Random House New Zealand Limited
18 Poland Road, Glenfield, Auckland 10, New Zealand

Random House South Africa
PO Box 2263, Rosebank 2121, South Africa

RANDOM HOUSE UK Limited Reg No. 954009

A CIP catalogue record for this book is available from the British library.

ISBN 0 099 26349 1

Printed in Singapore

THE WHALES' SONG

Story by Dyan Sheldon
Illustrations by Gary Blythe

Mini Treasures

RED FOX

L
ILLY'S grandmother told her a story.

'Once upon a time,' she said, 'the ocean was filled with whales. They were as big as the hills. They were as peaceful as the moon. They were the most wondrous creatures you could ever imagine.'

*L*ILLY climbed on to her grandmother's lap.

'I used to sit at the end of the jetty and listen for whales,' said Lilly's grandmother. 'Sometimes I'd sit there all day and all night. Then all of a sudden I'd see them coming from miles away. They moved through the water as if they were dancing.'

'*B*UT how did they know you were there Grandma?' asked Lilly. 'How would they find you?'

Lilly's grandmother smiled. 'Oh, you had to bring them something special. A perfect shell. Or a beautiful stone. And if they liked you the whales would take your gift and give you something in return.'

'WHAT would they give you, Grandma?' asked Lilly. 'What did you get from the whales?'

Lilly's grandmother sighed. 'Once or twice,' she whispered, 'once or twice I heard them sing.'

*L*ILLY'S uncle Frederick stomped into the room. 'You're nothing but a daft old fool!' he snapped. 'Whales were important for their meat, and for their bones, and for their blubber. If you have to tell Lilly something, then tell her something useful. Don't fill her head with nonsense. Singing whales indeed!'

'THERE were whales here millions of years before there were ships, or cities, or even cavemen,' continued Lilly's grandmother. 'People used to say they were magical.'

'People used to eat them and boil them down for oil!' grumbled Lilly's uncle Frederick. And he turned his back and stomped out to the garden.

*L*ILLY dreamt about whales.

In her dreams she saw them, as large as mountains and bluer than the sky. In her dreams she heard them singing, their voices like the wind. In her dreams they leapt from the water and called her name.

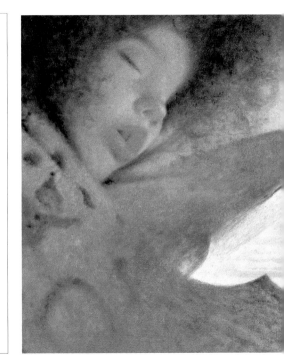

*N*EXT morning Lilly went down to the ocean. She went where no one fished or swam or sailed their boats. She walked to the end of the old jetty, the water was empty and still. Out of her pocket she took a yellow flower and dropped it in the water.

'This is for you,' she called into the air.

*L*ILLY sat at the end
of the jetty and waited.
   She waited all morning
and all afternoon.
   Then, as dusk began to
fall, Uncle Frederick came
down the hill after her.
'Enough of this foolishness,'
he said. 'Come on home.
I'll not have you dreaming
your life away.'

*T*HAT night, Lilly awoke
suddenly.

The room was bright
with moonlight. She sat up
and listened. The house
was quiet. Lilly climbed
out of bed and went to the
window. She could hear
something in the distance,
on the far side of the hill.

*S*HE raced outside and down to the shore. Her heart was pounding as she reached the sea.

There enormous in the ocean, were the whales.

They leapt and jumped and spun across the moon.

Their singing filled up the night.

Lilly saw her yellow flower dancing on the spray.

*M*INUTES passed,
or maybe hours.
Suddenly Lilly felt the
breeze rustle her
nightdress and the cold
nip at her toes. She
shivered and rubbed her
eyes. Then it seemed the
ocean was still again
and the night black
and silent.

Lilly thought she must
have been dreaming. She
stood up and turned for
home. Then from far, far
away, on the breath of
the wind she heard,
'Lilly! Lilly!'
The whales were
calling her name.

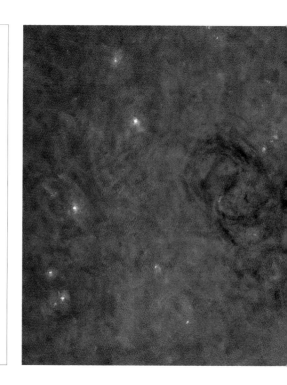